THE A+ CUSTODIAN

written by
louise borden

illustrated by
adam gustavson

MARGARET K. McELDERRY BOOKS • New York London Toronto Sydney

ALSO BY LOUISE BORDEN

The Little Ships: The Heroic Rescue at Dunkirk in World War II
Good Luck, Mrs. K.!
Sleds on Boston Common: A Story from the American Revolution
Fly High! The Story of Bessie Coleman
The Day Eddie Met the Author
Good-Bye, Charles Lindbergh
America Is . . .
Touching the Sky: The Flying Adventures of Wilbur and Orville Wright
Sea Clocks: The Story of Longitude
(Margaret K. McElderry Books)

For Ann Bobco,
an A+ friend—L. B.

For Mr. Shapiro and his
fourth-grade class,
with thanks—A. G.

Margaret K. McElderry Books
An imprint of Simon & Schuster Children's Publishing Division
1230 Avenue of the Americas, New York, New York 10020
Text copyright © 2004 by Louise Borden
Illustrations copyright © 2004 by Adam Gustavson
Book design by Sonia Chaghatzbanian
The text for this book is set
in Carre Noir Medium.
The illustrations are rendered in oil.
Manufactured in China
1 2 3 4 5 6 7 8 9 10

Library of Congress Cataloging-in-Publication Data
Borden, Louise.
The A+ custodian / Louise Borden ; illustrated by Adam Gustavson.
p. cm.
Summary: The students and teachers at Dublin Elementary School
make banners, posters, and signs for their school custodian to show
how much they appreciate him and all the work he does.
ISBN 0-689-84995-8
[1. Janitors—Fiction. 2. Schools—Fiction.] I. Title: A plus custodian
II. Gustavson, Adam, ill. III. Title.
PZ7.B64827 Aae 2004
[E]—dc21
2002012029

FIRST
EDITION

AUTHOR'S NOTE

custodian: one who has custody, as of a public building; a keeper; a guardian; (1775 –1785) a watchman.

Some school custodians are short. Some are tall. Some are thin and some are stout. Some are men and some are women. And they each have a name that is known to everyone in their schools. To adults their names are Arthur . . . or Eleanor . . . Fred . . . Dave . . . Sandy . . . Charlie . . . Irv . . . Flo . . . or James. To students they are Mr. Miller . . . or Mr. Iredale . . . Ms. Shriver . . . Mr. Fields . . . Mrs. Logan . . . Mr. Platt . . . or Mr. Ramrez. I'll bet every student at your school—even those in kindergarten!—knows your custodian's name.

In my school visits I have met hundreds of custodians in small country towns and big busy cities. They are there to greet me in the school gym or in the cafeteria. They set up microphones, plug in extension cords, line up chairs, and move tables. They give me their handshakes in welcome and place me in their care. I have listened to their voices and watched the details of their varied work.

Most of these wonderful custodians care very deeply about the students and teachers in their buildings. They watch kids grow up from kindergarten on. They watch new teachers grow into veteran teachers. They look at the student work hanging in the hallways, and they are proud of the learning that occurs in schools every day. They remember lots and lots of names. They eat birthday cupcakes, sometimes four in one day! When summer rolls around, they enjoy the quiet days in their buildings and work long hours to shine and wax floors and furniture so that on the first day of school, students and teachers and parents coming through those front doors will say, "WOW! Our school is ready for a new year!" Imagine . . . an A+ on the very first day of school.

Celebrate your custodian's hard work.

Best wishes . . .

Louisa Borden

John Carillo was the day custodian
at Dublin Elementary School.
Everyone liked Mr. Carillo:
the students . . .
the teachers . . .
Mrs. Greenwood, the school secretary . . .
the cooks . . .
the parents . . .
and Mr. Vance, the principal.

John Carillo had been the custodian
at Dublin Elementary for nineteen years,
and Mrs. Greenwood said she could count on one hand
the days that John had been sick
or missed work.

Every day
the short, stocky custodian
kept Dublin's hallways and rooms shiny clean
with his mops and his brooms
and his soaps and his polish.

And he had a key to every door and lock
at school.
Click cling jingle ring . . .
You could always hear the swing
of his keys
when Mr. Carillo headed down the hall
to the school office
or when he climbed up
one of his tall ladders
to replace a lightbulb
in the ceiling of the school gym.
Click cling jingle ring . . .
A good custodian always knew
which key fit the right lock.

Mr. Vance said John Carillo could fix anything,
and he was right about that.
Mr. Carillo knew about wiring and pipes
and windows and lights.
He was the man who had to keep
all the parts of the building
working in tip-top condition . . .
even the parts that were old and tired.

Mr. Carillo had two special closets,
all his own,
with big black letters on them:

CUSTODIAN

Those closets were crammed full of stuff:
buckets and old rags and damp sponges,
tools like hammers and pliers,
boxes of nails and screws,
and short and tall ladders
that clattered and screeched
whenever Mr. Carillo hauled one out
and carted it off down the hall
to some task.

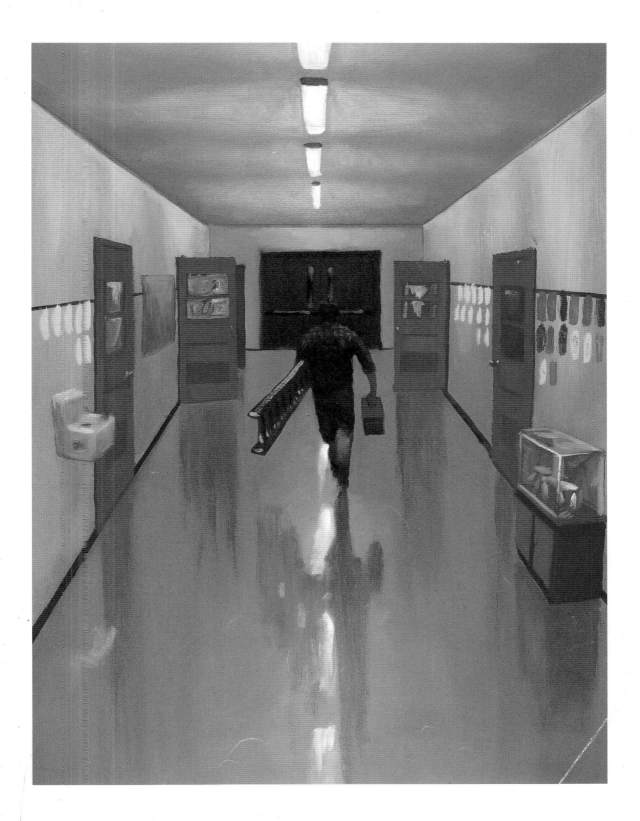

John Carillo was a jack of all trades:
If a second-grade teacher needed an extra desk
in her classroom,
or if a heavy table had to be moved
in the cafeteria,
or if a toilet overflowed
in the boys' bathroom,
people always hurried to the school office
and asked Mrs. Greenwood:
"Do you know where Mr. Carillo is?"
or asked:
"Say, have you seen John?"
Sometimes they just blurted out their words in a panic:
"Go find the custodian . . . quick!"

Every morning
John Carillo came to school in the pitch-black dark,
when most students were just waking up
or eating their breakfasts at home.
He unlocked the big red front doors
and switched on the lights
one by one by one by one
so that Dublin Elementary would look
cozy and bright,
even on the gloomiest days.

John Carillo wasn't a stylish man
in his flannel shirts
and his worn leather shoes.
But he was no ordinary janitor.
He was a custodian.

Gracie Sibberson
and her twin brother, Zach,
were third graders.

Their mother was a fifth-grade
teacher at Dublin,
and on many mornings,
when it was still dark outside,
Mrs. Sibberson and Gracie and Zach
arrived at school
soon after Mr. Carillo had unlocked
the front doors.

"Good morning, Mr. Carillo!"
the Sibbersons would call out
like the notes of a song
down the empty hall.
Then Mrs. Sibberson,
carrying her satchel full of papers and books,
would head to the teachers' workroom
for a mug of hot coffee.
Mr. Carillo brewed a big pot
each morning for the Dublin staff.
Every teacher thought John Carillo
made the best coffee in town.

"Morrrrrn-ing, you Early Birds,"
John would call back.
The echo of those words
always began the Sibbersons' school day.

Mrs. Sibberson told the twins:
"Mr. Carillo is an A+ custodian.
He uses a lot of elbow grease
so the school will run smoothly for others.
I think he loves every single brick
in this old building."

Dublin's custodian knew the names of all the students,
even the kindergartners.
Gracie didn't mind her nickname.
And neither did Zach.
No one else at school
had a special nickname like Early Birds.

While Mrs. Sibberson got ready for her fifth-grade day,
Gracie and Zach began to follow Mr. Carillo
around the building.
They watched him at his many tasks and asked:
"Can we help too?"

"Your Early Birds are no bother,"
the custodian told Mrs. Sibberson.
"They keep me company on these quiet mornings."
Then he winked at the twins and said:
"Annnnnnnnnnnnd if they do good work for me,
I'll bet I can rustle up a doughnut or two."
The twins liked the way
Mr. Carillo stretched out his words.

And that's how the Early Birds
became the school custodian's
Number One Assistants . . .
the year they were in third grade.

Zach became a whiz at tidying up
the forgotten lunch boxes and single mittens
in the Lost and Found bin.
He wiped sticky handprints
from the kindergarten tables,
and lugged a shipment of clay
to the art room.

Gracie carried boxes of school supplies
up the stairs to the fifth grade
and down the stairs to the first grade.
She untangled long extension cords
and counted out the traffic cones
before the big yellow buses arrived.

The twins took turns holding the dustpan
for Mr. Carillo's quick sweeps of his big broom.

There was always something that needed doing
somewhere in the building.

Before long
the Early Birds knew every Dublin classroom,
from the basement to the second floor—
what was different about them . . .
and what was the same.
Some were full of messy projects.
Some were orderly and neat.
Some had cages of snakes or gerbils
or guinea pigs or chicks just hatched.
The twins loved following Mr. Carillo
in his early morning work.
They loved being his assistants,
and they loved his doughnuts.

Sometimes
Mr. Carillo and the Early Birds
stood together in the quiet hallways
and looked at displays of student work
taped up on the long walls.

The custodian always beamed like a father
and said:
"I sure am proud of all you kids. . . .
You do terrrrrrr-i-fic work!"

Then he pointed up and down the hall.
"This whole building is my classroom."

One day
Gracie noticed something at Dublin Elementary
that she had never noticed before.
There were special words in every classroom
in different colors of ink . . .
words that were small on paper
but that meant something big.

The words were on spelling papers
and math quizzes,
on dinosaur poems
and homework pages.

Gracie puzzled over those words
from Monday to Thursday.
She thought about them while she was helping Mr. Carillo.
She thought about them
while she was waiting in line to go to recess.
And she thought about them
on the way to art,
and to music,
and to gym.

Finally Gracie told Zach
about all her hard thinking.
And she told her mom.
And then she told her third-grade teacher,
Mrs. Davis,
who told Mr. Vance.
And then the five of them had a top-secret meeting
in the principal's office
and made a wonderful plan.

Soon
everyone from kindergarten to fifth grade
at Dublin Elementary School
was whispering . . .

". . . our custodian . . ."
"Don't let him know . . ."
"Don't tell . . . don't tell . . ."
"SHHHH!"
". . . your best handwriting . . ."
". . . because we love Mr. Carillo . . ."
"Shhh . . ."

"... it's for our custodian ..."
"... get the tape and markers ..."
"... after school ..."
"Shh ... DON'T TELL Mr. Carillo ..."
"... Hurry ... tape it here ..."
"... It's for Mr. Carillo ..."
"Shh ..."
"... nobody tell ..."
"... it's top secret ..."

and they were working hard.

The next Monday
John Carillo arrived at school early in the morning
in the pitch-black dark.

He pulled out his ring of keys
and unlocked the big red front doors.
He began to switch on the lights
one by one by one by one.

It was then that he saw the wonderful banner
stretched across the main hallway:

As he slowly walked around his building,
John Carillo couldn't stop smiling.
He saw the important words
that Gracie Sibberson had thought about.
The words were everywhere . . .
in the handwriting of students and teachers . . .
on light switches . . . on door locks . . .
on heavy tables and extra desks . . .
in the boiler room . . .
and on the doors of the CUSTODIAN closets . . .
on buckets . . . on sponges . . . on ladders . . .
on the clean, shiny floors . . .
and on the railings of the stairwells . . .
on sink faucets . . . and up and down the hallways . . .
on all the old tired parts of the building . . .
and on the big coffee pot in the teachers' workroom . . .

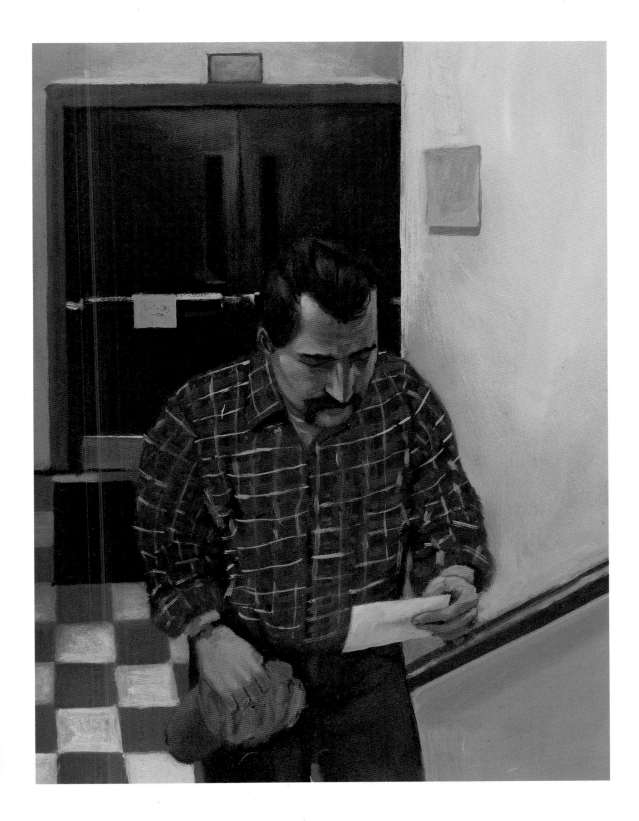

and he realized that this time
they had been written for him.

A+!

SUPER!

110%!

Excellent!

A+!

TERRIFIC!

Wow!

Dynamite!

Great Job!

Double Wow!

I LOVE This!

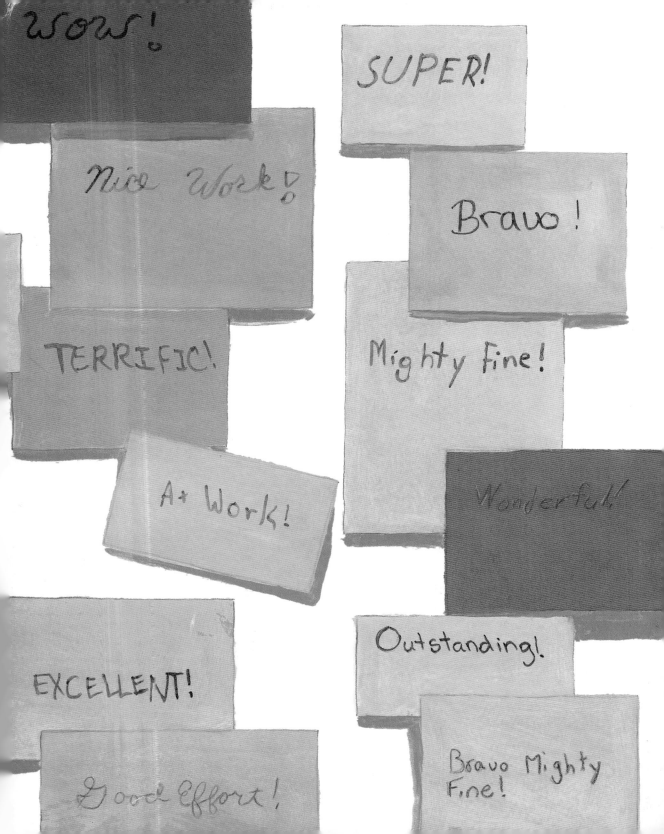

A little later that Monday morning
Mr. Carillo waited near the big banner
in the main hallway,
and Gracie and Zach Sibberson
stood proudly beside him.

Another week of school was about to begin.
The big yellow buses lined up
bumper to bumper
in front of Dublin Elementary,
the same as they always did,
with a *swish-hiss* of their brakes
and a *snap-flap* of their doors,
and the voices of four hundred Dublin students
filled up the shiny, clean lobby
like a rising tide.

"Mr. Carillo!" "Mr. Carillo!"
"Hey, Mr. Carillo!"

And in the midst of all the clamor
and celebration,
John Carillo leaned down
and whispered to Gracie and Zach:
"A fine building is mighty nice,
but it isn't much without the people inside it."

A pack of second-grade boys waved and yelled,
"Thank you, Mr. Carillo!"
as they hurried on by.
The Early Birds nodded and smiled.
Mr. Carillo sure knew a lot
about the care of their school.
He was an A+ custodian.